This book belongs to

....

Fun Ideas for the Storyteller

Are You Spring? is a gentle story about a funny misunderstanding – the kind that children will recognize and laugh at. They will also identify with Ulla's burning curiosity for an answer to her question.

Read on to find out how to get the most fun out of this story.

Zzzzzzzzz   Zzzzzzzz

GROWL!

Be a bear!

Snuggle up like Big Bear Mother and her cubs and have a good time with this book. Your child will love to join in with the noises in the story. *Snoooore* like sleeping bears; GROWL to scare away the wolves; and *buzzzzzzz* like bees doing their honey dance.

Now join in!

Let your child turn the pages. Point to the words as you read and encourage him to join in. The rhythm of the opening lines makes them especially fun to say. He will also want to call out repeated phrases like *"Are you Spring?"* Remembering a few key words or phrases like this one will really boost his confidence.

What season is it?

This story introduces the difficult concept of changing seasons. Talk with your child about weather and the seasons. What does he like best about each season? Talk about Ulla's feelings as she tries to be independent – feelings that your child will also be learning to understand.

Picture clues – can you spy the hare?

Ask your child to look at the pictures for clues as Winter turns to Spring. Notice how the colours change. What happens to the hare? Look at the animals – how do they survive in the cold? You might even talk about why bears hibernate. Don't worry if, like Ulla, your child doesn't quite understand.

Have a good time and enjoy the magic of the story!

Wendy Cooling

Wendy Cooling
Reading Consultant

For Barbara Buckley, who loved the Spring – CP
Help save the bears! Write to *The Raincoast Conservation Society, P. O. Box 26, Bella Bella, British Columbia V0T 1B0, Canada; ikrcoast@islandnet.com* – CW

Dorling **DK** Kindersley

LONDON, NEW YORK, SYDNEY, DELHI, PARIS, MUNICH and JOHANNESBURG

First published in Great Britain in 2000
by Dorling Kindersley Limited,
9 Henrietta Street, London WC2E 8PS

2 4 6 8 10 9 7 5 3 1

Text copyright © 2000 Caroline Pitcher
Illustrations copyright © 2000 Cliff Wright
The author's and illustrator's moral rights have been asserted.

A CIP catalogue record for this book is available from the British Library.

ISBN 0-7513-7213-7

Colour reproduction by Dot Gradations, UK

Printed in Hong Kong by Wing King Tong

Acknowledgements:
Series Reading Consultant: Wendy Cooling   Series Activities Advisor: Lianna Hodson
Photographer: Steve Gorton   Models: Sami, Anisa and Aziz Khan, Ryan Heaton

see our complete
catalogue at
www.dk.com

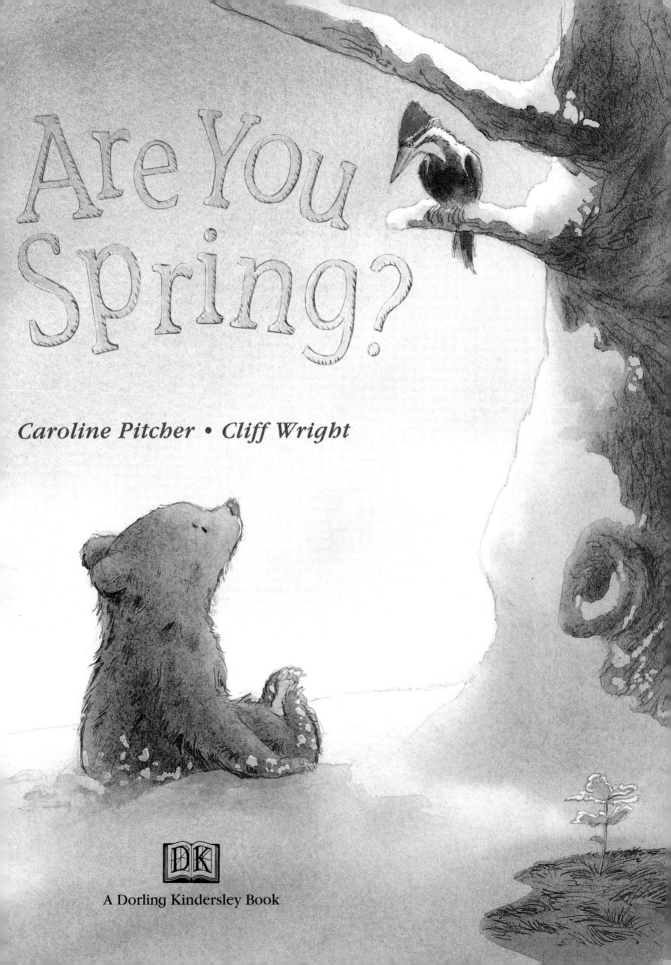

Are You Spring?

Caroline Pitcher • Cliff Wright

A Dorling Kindersley Book

Deep in the forest was the brown bears' den.
Deep in the den two cubs were born.
They slept and fed and fed and slept.

One day the she-cub sat up and said, "I want to go out there."

Big Bear Mother shook her head and said, "It's Winter, Ulla. Now go back to sleep like your good little brother."

Ulla scowled at her brother and said, "But when can I go out there?"

"When Spring comes," grunted Big Bear Mother.

So Ulla snuggled up and fell asleep wondering who Spring was.

A few days later Ulla woke up again.
She padded across the den and looked outside.

The snow dazzled her new little eyes.
"Shall I tell Spring to hurry up?" she called.
But Big Bear Mother didn't answer.
She was fast asleep, snoring.
Ulla was curious. She scampered
out of the den . . .

. . . and into the forest.

She saw a funny tree with two brown knobbly branches.

"Are you Spring?" she asked. "You've got big cloddy feet!"

"Those are my snowshoes," laughed Moose. "And I'm not Spring. But Spring is in the air when the trees sprout fresh leaves."

Ulla gazed up at the bright new leaves.

Tock-tock-tock, tock-tock-tock said someone up above.

"Are you Spring?" asked Ulla.

"No," said Woodpecker. "But Spring is coming when woodpeckers drum and birds build their nests."

Suddenly someone jumped out from behind a tree.

"Are you Spring?" cried Ulla. "You've got such sharp teeth."

"No," said Little Wolf. "I'm a cub."

"No you're not!" said Ulla. "I'm a cub and so is my brother, so I know what they look like!"

"You're a bear cub. I'm a wolf cub," explained Little Wolf.

A dark shadow fell across the snow.

Ulla looked up. There was another wolf cub, twenty times bigger.
"If you're Spring," she whispered, "I don't think I like you."

Then a voice Ulla knew growled, "Ulla! Quickly! Climb that tree!"

And Ulla found she could climb, quickly!
Big Bear Mother reared up and roared and
scared the wolves away.

Then she cried, "Ulla! Where have you been?
I woke up and you were gone!"

"Mum! I was so frightened on my own!
I was only looking for Spring . . ."

Big Bear Mother nuzzled Ulla and said,
"Spring will be here soon, but now it's time
to go home."

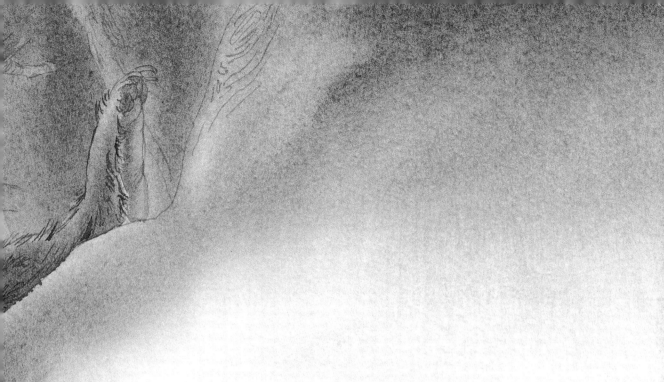

Back in the den, the bears cuddled in a cosy heap. Big Bear Mother said, "Snuggle up and listen to me, my cubs, and I will tell you stories of Spring."

Ulla and her brother snuggled up closer.

"Now, when Spring comes, the great snows melt. Rivers run fast. The fish leap high above the rocks, and I will teach you how to catch them . . ."

"Green leaves sprout on trees, wild flowers open in the grass, and blueberries swell, so juicy and purple, specially for bears to eat."

Big Bear Mother licked her lips.

"And, best of all, the bees buzz, doing their honey dance, up and down, round and round, leading us to their golden honey."

"Yummy!" cried Ulla, rolling and tumbling round the den. She couldn't wait for Spring to come!

So, night after night, snug inside their den,
the cubs listened to Big Bear Mother's tales.
Until Ulla couldn't wait any longer. "But who is
Spring?" she cried. "And when will she come?"

Big Bear Mother laughed. She padded to the
entrance of the den and looked out.

"This is Spring, Ulla!
Come and see her now.
She's here!"

Activities to Enjoy

If you've enjoyed this story, you might like to try some of these simple, fun activities with your child.

What's it like outside?

Look in magazines or photos for pictures of the seasons. Point out clues that indicate the season, such as golden leaves in Autumn. Ask your child to draw pictures of Spring, Summer, Autumn, and Winter, including his favourite things to do in each season. Write a simple sentence on each picture, then staple the pages together to make a book.

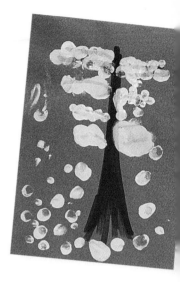

Cosy bear den

Your child can easily make a bear den by draping a sheet or blanket over some chairs or a table. Children will enjoy pretending to be Ulla Bear sleeping in the den or exploring the forest. What would Ulla Bear eat? What games would she play?

What's the weather?

Play a dressing-up game! Ask your child to put on the special clothes that he wears in the sun, snow, and rain.

Sprout seeds!

In the story, Moose tells Ulla, "*Spring is in the air when the trees sprout fresh leaves.*" Have fun sprouting some shoots of your own.

What you will need:
Paints or felt-tip pens; egg shells; cotton wool; watercress seeds; water.

Draw or paint faces on the broken egg shells. Keep them steady in an egg carton. Next, place wet cotton wool in the egg shells.

Sprinkle some watercress seeds over the cotton wool. Finally, place your egg shells on a window sill and keep the cotton wool moist.

Wait and watch as your faces grow green hair!

Other Share-a-Story titles to collect:

Not Now, Mrs Wolf!
by Shen Roddie
illustrated by Selina Young

The Caterpillar That Roared
by Michael Lawrence
illustrated by Alison Bartlett

Nigel's Numberless World
by Lucy Coats
illustrated by Neal Layton